DINOSAUR DAYS

TYRANNOSAURUS
The Tyrant Lizard

Benchmark Books
Marshall Cavendish Corporation
99 White Plains Road
Tarrytown, New York 10591-9001

Scientific consultant:
Rolf Johnson, Associate Curator of Paleontology;
Director, Science Media Center; Milwaukee Public Museum

Library of Congress Cataloging-in-Publication
Riehecky, Janet, date.
Tyrannosaurus : the tyrant lizard / Janet Riehecky
p.   cm -- (Dinosaur days)
Includes bibliographical references (p.   -   ) and index.
Summary: Describes a day in the life of a huge, meat-eating tyrannosaurus,
its behavior, environment, and its physical characteristics.
ISBN 0-7614-0601-8
1. Tyrannosaurus rex--Juvenile literature. [1. Tyrannosaurus rex.
2. Dinosaurs.] I. Title. II. Series: Riehecky, Janet, date. Dinosaur Days.
QE862.S3R543   1998   567.912'9--DC21   96-48540   CIP   AC

Printed in the United States of America

1 3 5 7 8 6 4 2

TYRANNOSAURUS
The Tyrant Lizard

WRITTEN BY JANET RIEHECKY
ILLUSTRATED BY SUSAN TOLONEN

BENCHMARK BOOKS

MARSHALL CAVENDISH
NEW YORK

4

The woods near the lake echoed with sounds. Birds called, insects buzzed, and creatures stirred the brush as they searched for food. But one sound stood out above the rest. It was a rumble—softer than thunder but just as threatening. It was the sound of a *Tyrannosaurus*'s stomach grumbling. He was hungry.

In a clearing nearby, *Edmontosaurus*, a duck-billed dinosaur, was also looking for food. She looked around cautiously and sniffed the air. Nothing. Feeling safe, she stretched her neck up and nibbled on some pine needles. They tasted so good, she didn't notice her herd moving farther and farther away. But *Tyrannosaurus* did.

Tyrannosaurus, the mighty "tyrant lizard," watched the duck-billed dinosaur from the shadow of an enormous magnolia tree. He stood upwind where the breeze would not carry his scent to the duck-billed dinosaur. He waited patiently. Only a slight twitching of his tail showed his eagerness to attack.

The duck-billed dinosaur moved to the next tree, and *Tyrannosaurus* had to make a decision. The duck-bill had chosen a tree farther away from *Tyrannosaurus*. If he waited, the duck-bill might move completely out of range. But if he charged now, the duck-bill was already far enough away that she might escape.

Tyrannosaurus's belly grumbled, and he made his decision. He charged. The duck-billed dinosaur heard the crash of branches breaking and the thud of *Tyrannosaurus*'s enormous feet. Then she saw the huge creature running toward her with his mouth open wide, revealing very long, very sharp teeth.

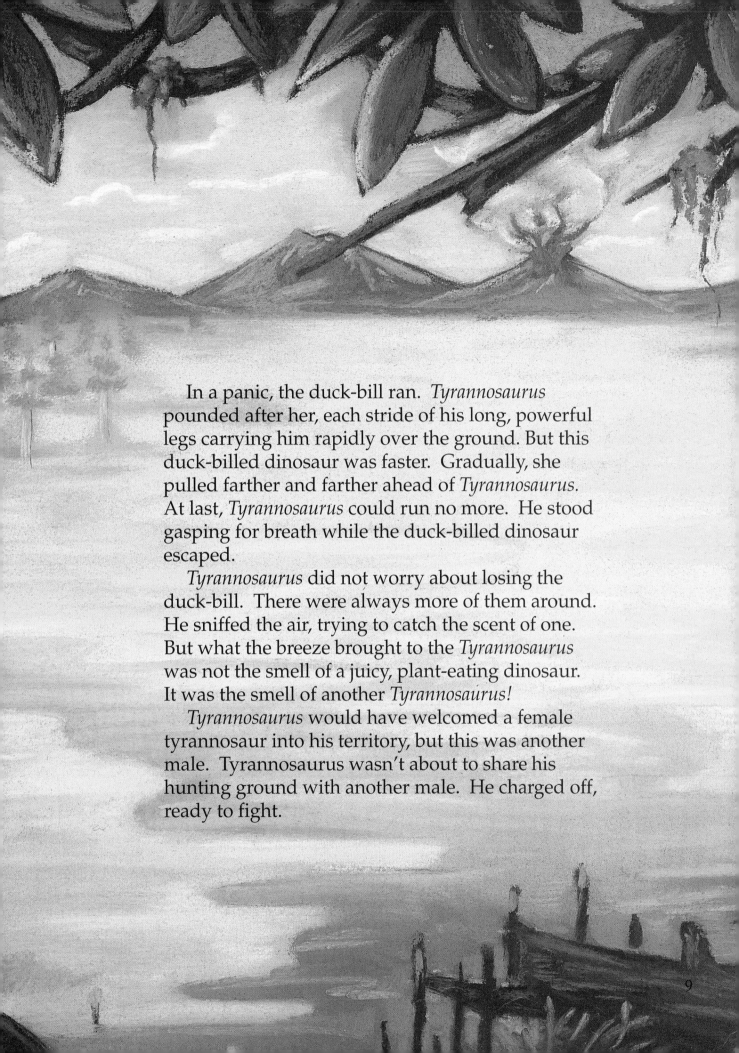

In a panic, the duck-bill ran. *Tyrannosaurus* pounded after her, each stride of his long, powerful legs carrying him rapidly over the ground. But this duck-billed dinosaur was faster. Gradually, she pulled farther and farther ahead of *Tyrannosaurus*. At last, *Tyrannosaurus* could run no more. He stood gasping for breath while the duck-billed dinosaur escaped.

Tyrannosaurus did not worry about losing the duck-bill. There were always more of them around. He sniffed the air, trying to catch the scent of one. But what the breeze brought to the *Tyrannosaurus* was not the smell of a juicy, plant-eating dinosaur. It was the smell of another *Tyrannosaurus*!

Tyrannosaurus would have welcomed a female tyrannosaur into his territory, but this was another male. Tyrannosaurus wasn't about to share his hunting ground with another male. He charged off, ready to fight.

The other tyrannosaur heard the approach of *Tyrannosaurus*, but he stood his ground—until he saw *Tyrannosaurus*.

The intruding tyrannosaur was not yet fully grown. He stood "only" twelve feet (3.7 meters) tall and stretched out "only" twenty-five feet (7.6 meters) long. Tyrannosaurus, on the other hand, *was* fully grown. He was eighteen feet (5.5 meters) tall and thirty-five feet (10.6 meters) long. He weighed five tons (4,536 kilograms). The intruding tyrannosaur wasn't ready for such an unequal fight. He left.

Tyrannosaurus didn't waste time chasing him. As long as the intruder left the area, *Tyrannosaurus* didn't care about him. He had more important things on his mind. Ah. He could smell something worth investigating close by.

Tyrannosaurus stalked silently toward a small clearing. But he was in for another disappointment. In the clearing stood *Ankylosaurus,* a large armored dinosaur, calmly chewing some leaves.

12

Tyrannosaurus liked the taste of armored dinosaurs, and he knew such a creature could not outrun him. However, there was a problem. The only soft spot on an armored dinosaur was its belly. And it wasn't easy to get to that belly.

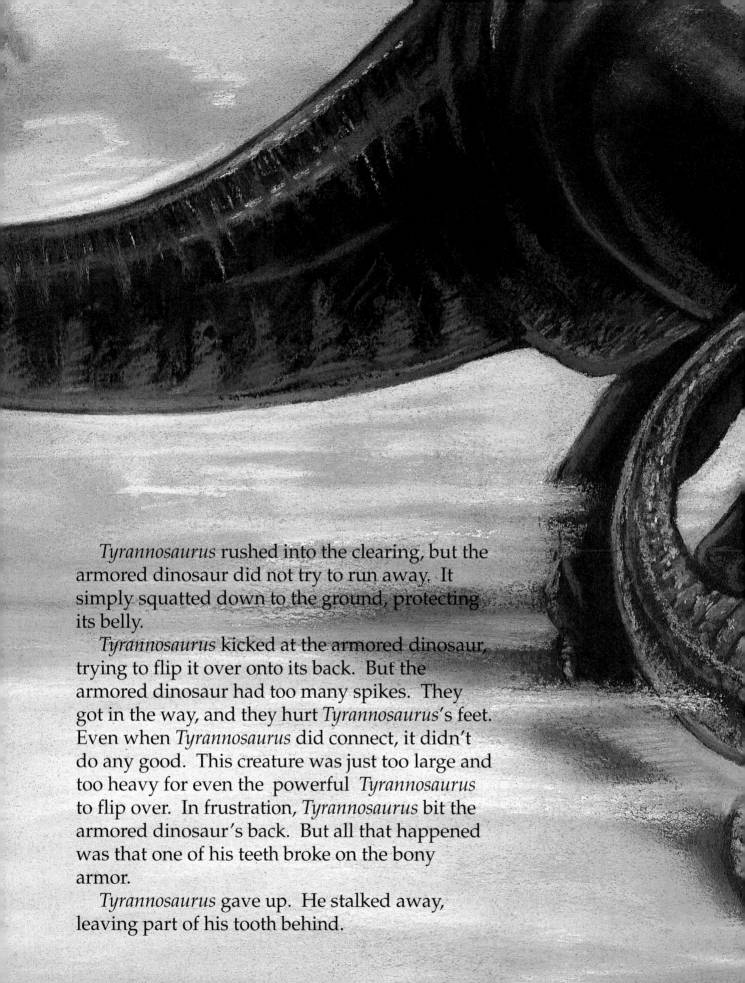

Tyrannosaurus rushed into the clearing, but the armored dinosaur did not try to run away. It simply squatted down to the ground, protecting its belly.

Tyrannosaurus kicked at the armored dinosaur, trying to flip it over onto its back. But the armored dinosaur had too many spikes. They got in the way, and they hurt Tyrannosaurus's feet. Even when Tyrannosaurus did connect, it didn't do any good. This creature was just too large and too heavy for even the powerful Tyrannosaurus to flip over. In frustration, Tyrannosaurus bit the armored dinosaur's back. But all that happened was that one of his teeth broke on the bony armor.

Tyrannosaurus gave up. He stalked away, leaving part of his tooth behind.

Tyrannosaurus passed the bones of a long-dead dinosaur. He sniffed around them. He didn't mind a meal that someone else had killed for him, but there wasn't anything left to this creature. Other scavengers had picked it clean.

A *Pteranodon* soared through the sky overhead. *Tyrannosaurus* ignored it. He knew he wasn't fast enough to catch it. But he did hope he would find something soon.

As *Tyrannosaurus* roamed about searching, he finally caught a scent. It was one of his favorite meals—*Triceratops*, a horned dinosaur.

Tyrannosaurus approached cautiously. He was hungry and didn't want this meal to get away. Soon, he caught a glimpse of the creature through the trees. It was a young horned dinosaur, and he was separated from his herd.

This time, *Tyrannosaurus* got lucky. The creature moved toward him, completely unaware of the danger he was walking into. *Tyrannosaurus* waited in ambush.

Triceratops took one step forward, then another. *Tyrannosaurus* lunged. The horned dinosaur gave a bellow of alarm and took off running, just as *Tyrannosaurus* had intended. Had *Triceratops* faced *Tyrannosaurus*, he would have been protected by the huge bony frill that covered his head and neck. Had he fought with his horns, he might have injured *Tyrannosaurus* and been able to get away. But when he ran away, *Tyrannosaurus* could slash at the side or back of the creature, where there was no protection.

20

Tyrannosaurus caught the young *Triceratops* easily. He sank his teeth into his side, then pulled back and waited. The wound was bleeding heavily and would soon kill the creature. But until he was dead, he was still dangerous. *Tyrannosaurus* had to be patient.

Triceratops staggered forward a few feet and then collapsed. *Tyrannosaurus* studied him a minute, then moved forward. At last he could fill his empty belly.

After his meal, *Tyrannosaurus* was tired.
He staggered away, not noticing the small
dinosaurs that had been attracted to the
smell of the dead *Triceratops*. They waited
until *Tyrannosaurus* was safely out of sight
before they began their feast.

Tyrannosaurus found a shady spot
under some pine trees and lay down.
Soon he was fast asleep. He slept many
hours, his belly comfortably full.

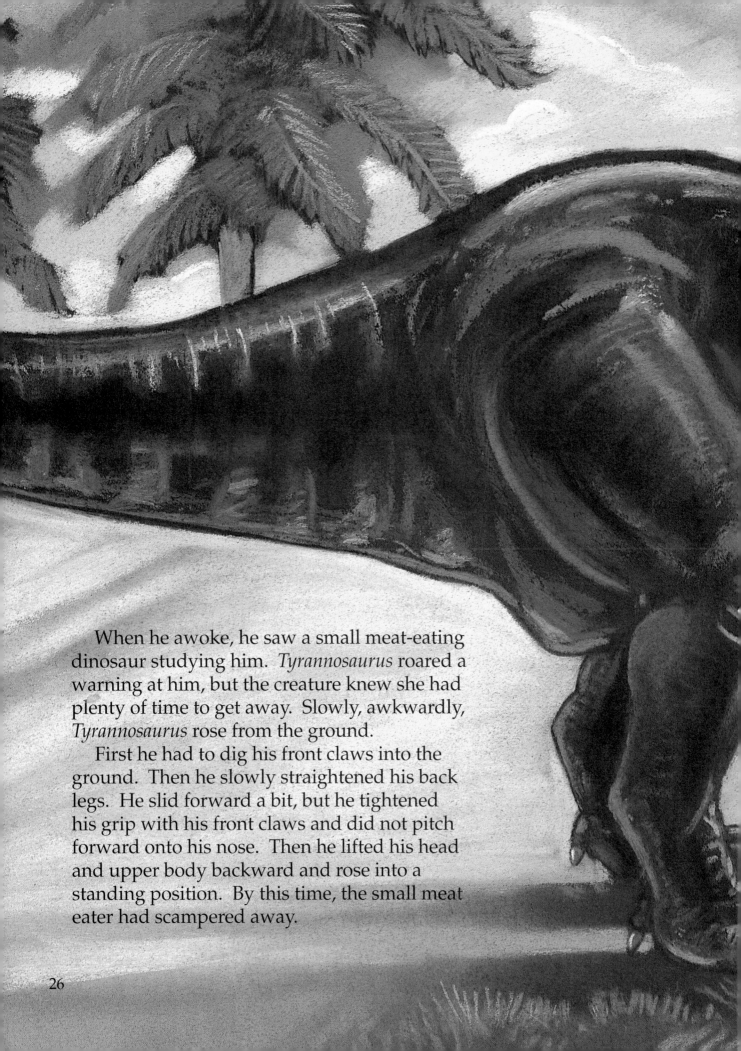

When he awoke, he saw a small meat-eating dinosaur studying him. *Tyrannosaurus* roared a warning at him, but the creature knew she had plenty of time to get away. Slowly, awkwardly, *Tyrannosaurus* rose from the ground.

First he had to dig his front claws into the ground. Then he slowly straightened his back legs. He slid forward a bit, but he tightened his grip with his front claws and did not pitch forward onto his nose. Then he lifted his head and upper body backward and rose into a standing position. By this time, the small meat eater had scampered away.

Tyrannosaurus stalked off into the
forest. He sniffed the air expectantly,
even though he wasn't really hungry yet.
Hmm. Something smelled interesting.
And it seemed to be quite close by. Might
as well check it out. *Tyrannosaurus*, the
tyrant lizard, was on the prowl again.

SOME FACTS ABOUT . . . TYRANNOSAURUS

Physical Appearance

Though scientists have just recently discovered meat-eating dinosaurs that may have been even bigger than the *Tyrannosaurus*, *Tyrannosaurus* is the largest meat-eating dinosaur about which much is known. Its name means "tyrant lizard," and it certainly was. Some scientists think the largest tyrannosaurs could grow twenty feet (6 meters) tall and fifty feet (15 meters) long and weigh seven tons (6,350 kilograms). These enormous creatures were built for killing. One of their most powerful weapons was their teeth. They were up to six inches (15 centimeters) long and sharp enough to slice through the toughest hide. It was just like having a mouthful of steak knives!

Tyrannosaurus also had powerful muscles. The muscles in its neck and jaws put power behind *Tyrannosaurus*'s bite. The powerful muscles in its legs could have helped it to chase its prey. Even the muscles in its tiny arms were strong enough to hold up to four hundred pounds (181 kilograms).

The claws of *Tyrannosaurus* were not as sharp as some of the other meat eaters' claws, but they didn't need to be. The two claws on each of its tiny arms could have sunk into a plant eater like meat hooks or could have been used to help the creature get up from the ground, as the *Tyrannosaurus* in the story does. The back claws could also have been used to attack a plant eater. And the kick *Tyrannosaurus* could put behind its back claws would have been able to kill some of the smaller plant eaters.

Lifestyle

No eggs of *Tyrannosaurus* have ever been found. Because so many other dinosaur eggs have been found, however, scientists believe *Tyrannosaurus* laid eggs, too. A creature as intelligent as *Tyrannosaurus* would have been capable of watching over its nest and taking care of its babies, but scientists have not yet found evidence of this.

Only one confirmed footprint of *Tyrannosaurus* has been found, so scientists can't use footprint evidence to tell whether tyrannosaurs moved in packs or lived by themselves. But all tyrannosaur skeletons have been found alone. Some scientists think this means tyrannosaurs lived by themselves most of the time or with just a mate. They may have claimed a territory and defended it against intruders, just as some meat-eating mammals do today. However, there is evidence of other big meat-eating dinosaurs living in packs and hunting together. *Tyrannosaurus* may have done that as well.

Scientists have recently discovered a nearly complete *Tyrannosaurus* skeleton in Montana. It includes many bones that have never before been found, including the bones of a complete arm. As scientists study this skeleton, they will be able to tell us more and more about the tyrant lizard—*Tyrannosaurus.*

GLOSSARY

ambush . . . . a surprise attack

duck-billed . . . . the common name of a group of dinosaurs that had long, flat heads, with
dinosaur snouts shaped like a duck's bill; some duck-billed dinosaurs had large bony crests on top of their skulls

frill . . . . a large bony plate that covered the neck and shoulders of ceratopsian dinosaurs

intruding . . . . . . coming into a place without being invited

scavenger . . . . . . an animal that finds animals that are already dead and eats them

scent . . . . smell; odor

territory . . . . an area of space that an animal claims as its own; it often includes the animal's nesting ground and/or hunting area

ton . . . . two thousand pounds (907.18 kilograms)

FOR FURTHER READING

Horner, John R. and Don Lessem. *The Complete T. Rex.* New York: Simon and Schuster, 1993.

Johnson, Rolf E. and Carol Ann Piggins. *Dinosaur Hunt!* Milwaukee: Gareth Stevens Children's Books, 1992.

Norman, David. *When Dinosaurs Ruled the Earth.* New York: Exeter Books, 1985.

Norman, David, and Angela Milner. *Eyewitness Books: Dinosaur.* New York, Alfred A. Knopf, 1989.

Pearce, Q. L. *Tyrannosaurus Rex and Other Dinosaur Wonders.* Englewood Cliffs, NJ: RGA Publishing Group, 1990.

Peterson, David. *Tyrannosaurus Rex: A New True Book.* Chicago: Children's Press, 1989.

Riehecky, Janet. *Tyrannosaurus.* Mankato, MN: The Child's World, 1988.

Stewart, Janet. *The Dinosaurs: A New Discovery.* Niagara Falls, NY: Hayes Publishing Co., 1989.

INDEX